# Puppies Online

## Treasure Hunt

By Jennifer Gray and Amanda Swift

GUINEA PIGS ONLINE

GUINEA PIGS ONLINE: FURRY TOWERS

GUINEA PIGS ONLINE: VIKING VICTORY

GUINEA PIGS ONLINE: CHRISTMAS QUEST

GUINEA PIGS ONLINE: BUNNY TROUBLE

# Puppies Online

## Treasure Hunt

### Jennifer Gray & Amanda Swift

#### with illustrations by Steven Lenton

Quercus

*For Anne and her dog, Jessie*
A.S.


*For Christine*
J.G.


*For nephew Jack (Russell) Lenton*
S.L.

First published in Great Britain in 2014 by

Quercus Editions Ltd
55 Baker Street
7th Floor, South Block
London
W1U 8EW

A CIP catalogue reference for this book is available
from the British Library

ISBN 978 1 84866 516 3
EBOOK ISBN 978 1 84866 517 0

1 3 5 7 9 10 8 6 4 2

Printed and bound in Great Britain by Clays Ltd, St Ives plc.

# Contents

# 1
# The Giant Breadstick

On a fine summer's day, a little brown puppy called Einstein was sitting on the back seat of a little black car, checking the details of his holiday on his owner's tablet computer.

'*New kennel in an old lighthouse,*' he read. '*Fresh food, lots of walks*

*and good company.*' He scratched his ear.
I hope it's a balanced diet, he thought.

Not far behind Einstein's car, Puzzle,
a big, fluffy, grey and white puppy,
leaned out of a window of a smart
grey saloon. As the car passed through
a sleepy seaside town he watched
a lollipop lady help some children
cross the road. She reminded Puzzle
of a criminal he'd once seen in a TV
detective show.

I wonder if she's
a part-time
gangster, he
thought.

Coming along
the road soon
after Puzzle was
a third car, with
a puppy called
Bounce inside it. She
was a black and white,

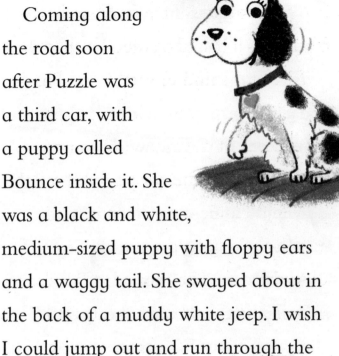

medium-sized puppy with floppy ears
and a waggy tail. She swayed about in
the back of a muddy white jeep. I wish
I could jump out and run through the
long grass, she thought.

A few minutes later the three cars
drew up outside a tall thin building on
a cliff. The puppies tumbled out.

'Wow! A giant breadstick!' said
Bounce.

'It's not a breadstick. It's a lighthouse,'
said Einstein.

'Where's the light then?' Bounce
asked.

'Maybe someone's stolen it,' said
Puzzle.

'No, it's just been turned off,' Einstein
explained. 'It's not needed any more.
Ships nowadays have their own
equipment to keep them away from
the rocks, and the lighthouse has been
turned into a kennels instead.'

'Oh,' said Bounce. 'Do you want

4

to play?' she asked, giving Einstein a friendly lick.

'I might want to play,' said Einstein, moving away, 'but if someone's going to lick me I like to know their name first.'

'I'm Bounce,' said Bounce. 'I'm a springer spaniel. Who are you?'

'Einstein.' He puffed out his chest. 'I'm a very clever dachshund. I'm named after a famous scientist who . . .'

Einstein didn't finish his sentence because Bounce had bounced off to say hello to the third puppy. Einstein trotted over to join them.

'I'm Puzzle,' said Puzzle. 'And if you're so clever –' he turned to Einstein – 'what type of dog am I?'

'An Old English sheepdog,' Einstein said immediately.

'You don't look old,' said Bounce to Puzzle.

'I'm not. I'm a puppy like you,' Puzzle said.

'So why are you called "old"?' asked Bounce.

'I'm not. I'm called Puzzle.'

'Did you know Old English sheepdogs date from—' Einstein began.

But once again he didn't get a

chance to finish what he was saying. This time it was because a girl who looked about nine ran up to the puppies and tried to cuddle them all at once. Einstein thought *she* might be interested in the history of sheepdogs, but then he remembered that although puppies could understand what humans said, humans couldn't understand what puppies barked.

'Here you are at last! I'm so excited to see you!' said the girl. 'I'm Jackie. I'm staying with my grandad all week so I can help look after you.' Einstein brushed his head against her ankle.

She laughed and bent down to stroke his silky coat. 'You must be Einstein.' She looked at his collar and smiled. 'What a smart collar! I've never seen one with a bow tie before.'

She turned to Puzzle and gave his head a pat. 'And fluffy Puzzle! What a long fringe you have. I'd better trim it while you're here, or else you might not be able to see where you're going and fall in a cowpat!'

Bounce's owner had brought a tin of dog biscuits. Bounce grabbed one of the biscuits and dropped it at Jackie's feet, as if it was a present. Jackie picked it up, ruffled Bounce's fur and said, 'Thank you, Bounce.'

'I hope she doesn't eat it,' said Einstein. 'It's been in Bounce's mouth. It wouldn't be very hygienic.'

'Welcome to Sandcliff Lighthouse,' said an old man as he came out of the front door. 'I'm Jackie's grandad Trevor, ex-lighthouse keeper and current keeper of the kennels.'

'He looks more like a smuggler to me,' said Puzzle, and then bounded off to explore the lighthouse while the puppies' owners chatted to Trevor and Jackie. Bounce rushed after Puzzle.

'Wait for me!' Einstein followed as fast as he could, which was still quite slow as his legs were so short.

On the ground floor of the lighthouse was a big kitchen and

living space. The first floor had a
bathroom and two little bedrooms –
one for Jackie, one for Trevor. On the
second floor there was one big room
with three baskets, each lined with
material as soft as the puppies' fur.
Above each basket was a photo of
their owner, and next to the baskets
there was a box of dog toys.

Best of all, the lighthouse had a long
slide that wound from the second floor
all the way down to the ground floor.

'This is amazing!' said Bounce,
trying out her basket.

'One thing I want to know is why

there are only three dogs here. It's not much of a kennels,' said Puzzle.

'It's probably because they've only just opened—' Einstein began.

'What *I* want to know,' Bounce interrupted, 'is, if this used to be a lighthouse, what have they done with the light?'

'If you'll stop interrupting me I'll tell you!' Einstein said.

'It's on the ceiling, like most lights,' said Puzzle, looking up.

'I don't mean the light for this room,' said Bounce. 'I mean the big light, the one that showed the ships the way.'

'I'll tell you about that after tea,' said Einstein as he marched over to have a closer look at the toys.

'I bet you're saying that because you don't know where it is,' said Puzzle.

'Yes, I do,' Einstein said.

'No, you don't.'

'Yes, I do!'

Just then a square shape in the corner of the ceiling caught Puzzle's attention. He forgot about squabbling with Einstein. 'Look!' he said. 'It's a trapdoor!'

# 2
# "Cowpat"

The puppies looked up. The trapdoor
was at the top of a set of wooden stairs.
The stairs looked as if they hadn't been
used in a while, and the handrail was
covered in dust.

The three puppies crept carefully
up the steps. When they got to the
top Puzzle stood on his hind legs and
pushed hard at the trapdoor with his

front paws. It gave a creak, then opened with a bang.

'Follow me,' he said, 'but be careful. Criminals might be lying in wait.'

'What criminals?' Bounce whispered.

'I don't know,' Puzzle said. 'I just learned to say that because my owner is a police detective and we watch a lot of crime shows on TV.'

Puzzle heaved himself through the trapdoor. Bounce followed, springing lightly after him. They landed in a pool of sunshine in a big, bright room. The two puppies blinked.

'Hmmm, just as I thought!' Puzzle

said. 'The criminals' hideout.'

The room was round like theirs,
but it had glass windows all the
way round instead of walls. On the
side facing the sea was a bank of
machinery with lots of switches and
dials and a computer screen set up on
a counter.

'It's not a criminals' hideout,' Bounce said. 'It's a control centre for launching spaceships.'

'What makes you so sure?' Puzzle asked.

'My owner is a stuntwoman,' replied Bounce. 'She's in loads of action films. We watch them together when they come out on DVD.'

They heard a scrabbling on the stairs. It was Einstein. 'Can someone give me a paw up?' he shouted. 'I can't reach.'

Puzzle leaned over the edge of the trapdoor and hauled him up.

'Be careful with my collar!' Einstein yelped. He dusted himself off and started sniffing about.

'It's a criminals' hideout,' Puzzle explained.

'No, it's not. It's a control centre for launching spaceships,' Bounce told him.

'You're both wrong.' Einstein held up a paw for silence. 'There's a more scientific explanation for what happens in this room.' He sniffed about. 'You need to think about the information.'

'What do you mean?' asked Bounce.

'Well,' said Einstein, 'my owner is an archaeologist. She goes on digs to look for things underground that tell us about people in the past.'

'Like bones?' Bounce asked.

'Yes,' said Einstein. 'Exactly.'

'I look for bones underground. Does that make me an archaeologist?' asked Puzzle.

'No,' said Einstein firmly. 'Definitely not. Now listen.' He pointed with his paw at some marks on the floor. 'These were made by a pair of size-ten Wellington boots. There's a trace of sheep's dropping on the right heel.'

Puzzle and Bounce stared hard at the tiled floor. Sure enough it was criss-crossed with faint muddy boot prints.

'I saw a pair of size-ten Wellingtons in the boot rack downstairs when we arrived.' Einstein paused. 'They belong to Trevor.'

'So Trevor's a criminal?' Puzzle frowned. 'I thought he was acting suspiciously.'

'Or an astronaut?' Bounce suggested.

'No!' Einstein said, exasperated. 'He's an ex-lighthouse keeper. This is where Trevor used to do his job. The information tells us that this is the control room for the light.'

'That's so cool!' Bounce scampered about the room. She stopped. 'But I still want to know – where *is* the light?'

'Above us,' Einstein explained. 'It can't be in the control room because it's too bright.'

'I wish we could turn it on,' Bounce said. 'It would be really fun to play with all those switches.'

'I know! We could make a den in here,' Puzzle suggested. 'We could set it up as our HQ for when we're solving crimes.'

'You don't know that there *are* any crimes,' Einstein said.

'There's crime everywhere,' Puzzle said. He opened one of the cupboards, pulled out a pair of binoculars and jumped up on the chair. He leaned on the counter with his paws, and looked through the binoculars. 'Aha,' he said. 'Just as I thought: the criminals' hideout.'

'Where?' Bounce sprang on to the swivel chair next to him and spun round and round until Puzzle stopped her.

'Over there, on the island.'

A little way out to sea was a small island, covered in grass and trees. A sandy beach curved around a bay. At one end was a large white house built on top of some rocks.

'You can reach it along that path through the sea,' Puzzle said. 'It's the perfect getaway for a criminal.'

'Stop going on about criminals,' said Einstein. 'You have no information that it's a perfect getaway.'

'Well, you stop going on about information,' Puzzle retorted. 'You have no information that it isn't!'

'How come there's a path through the sea anyway?' Bounce asked.

'It's called a causeway,' Einstein shouted up. 'At high tide it's covered by water.'

'Let's see!' Bounce said.

Puzzle passed her the binoculars.

Bounce looked through them. 'Oh yes,' she said. 'There it is. It runs all the way from the lighthouse to the island.'

'I want to see!' Einstein yapped, jumping up and down.

But he didn't get to see, at least not at that particular moment, because Jackie called them down to have their tea.

Einstein went across to the trapdoor, lowered his back legs carefully over the edge and dropped down on to the top step.

Bounce bounded after him.

Puzzle came last, carefully closing the trapdoor behind him.

'Do you think we should show Jackie that we've found the control room?' Einstein asked.

'No, I don't,' Puzzle said. 'She might tell Trevor, and he might not let us go up there any more. That's why there's a trapdoor – to stop anyone going in. I know! We should think of a password.

Then if someone comes up when one of us is up there on our own, we know whether or not to hide.'

'What about "archaeology"?' Einstein suggested.

'Or "bones"?' Bounce said.

'I found it, so I get to choose.' Puzzle thought for a minute. 'Cowpat,' he said eventually.

Bounce pulled a face. 'Cowpat?'

'Yes, because they're smelly and I like rolling in them. No one will ever guess that.'

'I wouldn't be too sure,' Einstein muttered under his breath.

'Race you down the slide!' Bounce cried.

And the three puppies whizzed down the slide one after the other to have their tea.

# 3
# Digging for Victory

Bounce was the first to wake up the next morning. The sun was streaming through the window. She bounced out of her basket and started barking. 'Come on, guys, let's go exploring.'

'What time is it?' Puzzle asked sleepily.

Einstein opened one eye. 'Five minutes past seven,' he said.

'How do you know that?' Bounce

asked, impressed. 'Can you tell the time from the sun?'

'I can,' Einstein said. 'But I didn't. There's a clock on the wall.' He closed his eye. 'Now pipe down. I need my brain sleep.'

'Brain sleep?' Bounce repeated.

'Yes. It's like beauty sleep only for brainy dogs like me,' Einstein said. He started to snore. But Einstein wasn't to get any more brain sleep that morning because just then the puppies heard Jackie calling them for breakfast.

After they had all eaten, Jackie pulled on her trainers and grabbed her backpack. 'Come on, puppies,' she said, 'we're going for a walk.' She opened a drawer and pulled out the three leads the puppies' owners had left the day before. Einstein's lead was blue, Bounce had a red one and Puzzle's had once been white but was now grey and muddy, like most of his coat. Jackie clipped them on to the puppies' collars.

Trevor was doing the washing-up.

'See you later, Grandad,' Jackie called.

The puppies milled around her feet, getting tangled up in each other's leads.

Trevor dried his hands. 'Where are you off to?' he asked, bending down to untangle the dogs.

'The beach,' Jackie replied. 'It's the sandcastle competition today!'

'That sounds fun.' Trevor had straightened out the leads. He opened the front door.

'I don't want to be on a lead,' barked Bounce. 'I want to run about.'

'So do I,' barked Puzzle. 'I want to roll in a cowpat.'

'In that case we need a plan,' Einstein yapped. 'We need to get tangled up again. Then Jackie will let us off.'

'Good idea,' the others agreed.

As soon as they were outside, Bounce jumped in front of Puzzle, Puzzle tripped over Einstein, and Einstein got his foot caught on Puzzle's lead and fell over.

'Oh no!' Jackie cried. 'We'll never get anywhere at this rate! Maybe I should just let them off the lead.'

'All right,' Trevor agreed.

Jackie unclipped the puppies' leads.

'I told you!' Einstein barked to his friends as they raced off through the grass.

'Watch out for Mrs Bossy though,' Trevor called after Jackie. 'You know what she's like about dogs. Make sure the puppies don't go near her garden.'

'I will,' Jackie called back.

The puppies hardly heard her. They were too excited. They scampered about, sniffing all the lovely seaside smells. Even Einstein, who didn't usually like walks, was enjoying himself. He wanted to find the sheep's dropping that matched the one he'd sniffed out in the control room so that he could work out how long it had been on Trevor's boot.

'This way!' Jackie led them along a narrow path that skirted the cliffs next to the lighthouse. 'Don't go too near the edge!' she warned.

Puzzle decided to investigate anyway. He went right up to the fence and looked down. The tide was out and the land fell away in a sheer drop to the dangerous rocks below.

'Puzzle!' Jackie called. 'I told you not to go there. Come here!'

Puzzle backed away from the edge and returned to the path.

'That was scary!' he said to Bounce and Einstein.

'Why did you do it then?' Einstein asked.

'I thought there might be some smugglers down there,' Puzzle said.

Einstein rolled his eyes.

After a little while the path dipped down towards a sandy beach.

'Hooray, I can go swimming!' Bounce cried.

'And I can have an ice cream!' Puzzle shouted.

'And I can read somebody's book!' said Einstein.

The sea was dotted with little colourful boats. 'That one's Grandad's,' Jackie said, pointing to a small blue-and-white-painted boat. 'I'll take you out on it tomorrow if you like.'

Bounce and Puzzle wagged their tails to show that they *would* like. Einstein wasn't so sure. He thought he might get seasick. He was certainly getting tired. His legs were much shorter than the others'. He sat down for a rest.

'What's the matter?' asked Bounce.

'Nothing,' Einstein said. He didn't want them to know he was tired. 'I'm just looking at the boats.'

Jackie picked him up. 'We'd better hurry,' she said. 'We don't want to miss the sandcastle competition.' She dashed along the beach past a line of pretty cottages. The cottages were all painted different colours. Jackie pointed at a yellow one with a beautiful garden with a big oak tree in it and flower beds full of lupins.

'Whatever you do,' Jackie said, 'don't go in there. It's Mrs Bossy's garden. She hates dogs.'

There were already lots of children on the beach making sandcastles.

'This looks fun!' said Bounce, wagging her tail madly to show Jackie she was excited.

'We'll go here.' Jackie picked a spot a little way away from the sea. She threw her backpack on to the sand, unfastened the Velcro, tipped the backpack upside down and shook it. Buckets and spades tumbled out. 'All right, puppies,' she said. 'I'll fill the buckets.' She picked up the buckets and a spade and went off to the water's edge to find wet sand for their castle.

'I'll make a plan,' Einstein said. He began marking the castle out on the sand with pebbles and twigs. It was a rather complicated design, involving a moat, four round towers and a keep in the middle. 'Do you think it's big enough?' he asked.

'Only if you're very small,' said Bounce.

'I'll investigate what everyone else is doing,' Puzzle said, 'and make sure they're not cheating. I'll be back in a minute.' He wandered off.

'I'll dig the moat.' Bounce used her four paws to dig a very big channel around the castle and down to the sea.

A few minutes later Jackie came back with her buckets of wet sand. She plonked them down. Einstein was just trying to explain his plan to her by barking and wagging his tail when a boy's voice interrupted him.

'Is this your dog?' the boy said.

Einstein and Bounce looked up. So did Jackie.

The boy was about Jackie's age. He had Puzzle with him on the end of a piece of string.

'Yes!' Jackie gave Puzzle a hug. 'Where have you been, you naughty thing?'

'In Gran's garden,' the boy said. He pointed to the yellow cottage just behind the beach. A thin woman with a long nose and half-moon spectacles was standing beside the gate, shaking her fist at them.

'Mrs Bossy!' Jackie gasped. 'Oh no! What was he doing?'

'Digging up the flower beds,' the boy said. 'Gran wasn't very pleased.'

'I'm really sorry,' Jackie said, taking the string. 'I told him not to. I was so busy making the sandcastle, I didn't realize he'd gone!'

'It doesn't matter. Gran's always complaining about something.' The boy grinned. He hesitated then added, 'Can I help you build the sandcastle? I like dogs.'

'OK,' Jackie said. 'I'm Jackie.'

'I'm Bradley,' said the boy.

'Where do you live?' asked Jackie.

'Just along the coast,' Bradley replied. 'My parents own a hotel. They're really busy at the moment so I've been spending quite a lot of time at my gran's.'

The two children chatted happily as they went about their work.

The puppies had been sitting in a line, watching the children make friends.

'He seems really nice,' Bounce said.

'I don't think we can trust him,' Puzzle grumbled. 'I didn't like the way he just grabbed hold of me. Maybe we should check if he's got a criminal record.'

'He was trying to help!' Einstein said. 'What were you doing in Mrs Bossy's garden anyway? You were supposed to be investigating the other sandcastles.'

'No, I wasn't.'

'Yes, you were.'

'No, I wasn't.'

'What's got into them?' Bradley asked.

'I don't know,' Jackie said. She giggled. 'Wouldn't it be funny if they were actually having a conversation and we didn't know?'

Just then there was a commotion

at the other end of the beach. The puppies stopped arguing. They stared in astonishment. A huge digger on giant tractor wheels was crawling along the beach towards them, squashing everyone's sandcastles! The digger stopped just a little way from them. A man jumped out of the cab of the digger and started to inspect the sand.

'He's very tall,' Bounce said.

Einstein craned his neck to look the man up and down. 'That's because he's wearing platform shoes,' he said.

'He's very fat,' Puzzle said.

'That's because he's wearing a padded coat,' Einstein said.

'He's got huge hair.' Bounce stood on her hind legs to get a better look at it.

'That's because he's wearing a wig,' Einstein said.

The children put down their spades. They watched the digger in amazement.

'Who is he?' Jackie asked Bradley.

The puppies listened intently.

'His name's Mike Dodger,' Bradley said. 'Gran says he's a troublemaker. He lives on the island opposite Sandcliff Lighthouse.'

'I knew it!' Puzzle barked excitedly. 'I told you it was a criminals' hideout!'

'You don't *know* he's a criminal,' Einstein said immediately.

'He must be,' Bounce said. 'Otherwise he wouldn't be digging up the beach at a kids' sandcastle competition.'

Mike Dodger was now digging huge scoops of sand and plonking them in a pile. He had already made quite a big hole that didn't look anything like a sandcastle.

'What's he doing that for?' Jackie asked Bradley.

Bradley shrugged. 'Search me!' he said.

The puppies glanced at one another. They intended to find out just what Mike Dodger was up to.

# 4
# The Treasure Map

'Leave this to me,' said Bounce. Before anyone could stop her, she dashed towards the digger and lay down in its path.

'Get out of my way!' Mike Dodger shouted at her.

'Bounce!' Jackie called. 'Come back!'

But Bounce didn't move a muscle.

'I don't like the look of this,' Puzzle said.

'He's bound to stop,' Einstein said. 'Isn't he?'

'Don't bank on it.' Puzzle shook his head. 'You don't understand the workings of the criminal mind. He's going to run her over. Come on!' He rushed after Bounce.

Einstein scampered after Puzzle.

The two puppies barked up at the cab, where Mike Dodger sat behind the wheel.

'Woof! Woof! Woof!'

'Yap, yap, yap.'

'Stop yapping,' Mike Dodger shouted as the digger moved forward.

'It's not working!' Einstein said. The digger's front wheels were getting really close to Bounce.

'There's only one thing for it!' Puzzle bounded forward, grabbed Bounce's collar in his jaws and dragged her out of the path of the digger.

Bounce lay on the sand, panting. 'What did you do that for?' she demanded.

'You were going to get run over!' Puzzle replied.

'No, I wasn't. I would have jumped out of the way,' said Bounce crossly. 'I wanted to stop the digger from knocking over our sandcastle. And now look!'

The digger was almost on top of Jackie and Bradley's sandcastle.

'Stop!' shouted Bradley, holding up his hand.

'No way! I haven't finished yet!' Mike Dodger shouted back.

'If you don't stop, I'll go and get the lifeguard. Diggers aren't allowed on the beach!'

The digger stopped.

'I hate kids!' Mike Dodger muttered under his breath. 'And dogs.' He gave the puppies a nasty look.

'You're staying up at Sandcliff Lighthouse, aren't you?' he said to Jackie.

'What's that got to do with you?' said Jackie.

'I'm going to report these dogs of yours,' Mike snapped back. 'They nearly caused a serious accident here. They're not safe. And you shouldn't be looking after unsafe dogs. I could get your kennels shut down.'

'You can't do that!' shouted Bradley.

'It's OK, Bradley.' Jackie touched him lightly on the arm and whispered something to him. 'It's not worth it.'

'You're right,' said Bradley. 'Let's ignore him.'

So they turned and went back to working on their sandcastle. Bounce went back to digging the moat. Einstein and Puzzle watched as Mike Dodger reversed the digger away from them. Then they trotted over to talk to Bounce.

'Wow!' said Puzzle when he saw the deep channel. 'You'll hit Australia in a minute!'

'Now you really *are* being unscientific,' said Einstein crossly.

'No, I'm not,' said Puzzle. 'Australia is on the other side of the world.'

'Yes, but you can't dig through the earth's core. It's too hot.'

'I'll tell you what's too hot – me!' said Bounce, flopping down on her tummy for a rest in the shade. As she landed she felt something hard beneath her. She tapped it with her paw.

'There's something here,' she said to the other two.

'Maybe it's New Zealand,' suggested Puzzle.

'It's not big enough to be a country,' answered Bounce, scraping sand away.

The other two puppies peered into the sandy hole, trying to work out what it was. As she scraped they could all see something that looked like a tin of biscuits.

'Biscuits!' said Bounce, recognizing her favourite food. 'A tin of biscuits!' She pulled it out of the hole with her front paws. 'I get to choose first 'cause I found them.'

'They're not dog biscuits,' said Einstein, sniffing them.

'Maybe they're human ones,' said Puzzle, drooling. 'I once ate a whole packet of ginger-nut biscuits. They made me sneeze, but they were delicious.'

Bounce cleared all the sand away from the tin and tried to wriggle the lid off with her paws. It was jammed shut. So she picked up the tin in her mouth and bounced over to where Jackie and Bradley were writing their names in the sand next to their finished sandcastle. Puzzle and Einstein followed.

'Biscuits!' exclaimed Jackie, picking up the tin that Bounce had dropped at her feet. 'I'm starving! Where did you get them from, Bounce?'

'Maybe she pinched them from someone's picnic,' suggested Bradley.

'It looks too old for that,' said Jackie, examining the rust on the tin. She tried to prise it open.

The puppies flared their nostrils, ready to breathe in the delicious smell of biscuits.

'Let me do it,' said a man's voice. A large hairy hand snatched the tin from Jackie.

The puppies looked up in surprise.
The hand belonged to Mike Dodger.

Jackie's face fell. 'Oh. It's you.'

'Yes, it is me. Mike Dodger. Dodger
by name, dodgy by nature.' Mike Dodger
grasped the edge of the biscuit-tin lid
with his nails and pulled it off as fast as
he could.

'It's not fair if he gets the biscuits!'
Bounce protested. 'It's rude and greedy
all at the same time. We should stop him!'

'Grrrrrr . . .' Einstein growled at Mike Dodger.

'Woof! Woof! Woof!" Puzzle barked at him.

'Chomp!' Bounce grabbed his trouser leg.

'Get off me, you mangy brutes!' Mike Dodger shouted at the puppies. He staggered backward and fell into Bounce's moat.

The children giggled and the puppies crowded around. Mike Dodger was up to his armpits in soggy sand. He put the tin down on the dry sand beside the hole. The puppies looked

longingly into the tin, but there were
no biscuits inside, only an old, tattered
piece of paper with pictures on it.

'Where are the biscuits?' asked Jackie.

'Biscuits?! Forget biscuits!' Mike Dodger cried. 'This is what I was looking for. At last, after all these years! The treasure map!'

*Treasure map?!* Puzzle and Bounce pricked up their ears. Einstein started fiddling with his bow tie.

Mike Dodger pulled himself out of the hole, put the lid back on the biscuit tin, clutched the tin to his chest and clambered back up on to his digger as fast as his platform shoes would allow.

'Hey! Wait a minute!' Jackie called after him. 'My puppy found that tin: we want to look at what's inside!'

'Give that back!' shouted Bradley. He chased Mike along the beach, Jackie and the puppies following, but the engine started to roar and none of them managed to catch up with Mike before he trundled off towards the sea's edge.

'You'll never catch me!' Mike called back at them. The digger slid into the water.

'What's he doing?' Jackie asked in astonishment. 'The digger will sink!'

'We'll get him now! He can't swim!' shouted Bradley. 'I've seen him wearing armbands at the local pool.'

But as the digger went further into the water it didn't sink. Instead, an inflatable rubber cushion appeared around the base of the cab and the digger began to float. It had converted into a boat! Mike Dodger sat safe and dry in the cab as the 'diggercraft' set off towards his island. The puppies sat watching in a row on the beach, their jaws open and their tongues panting. They'd never seen a digger that could float before!

Bradley gave up the chase. 'It's not
fair that he took the treasure map when
the puppies found it,' he said, returning
to the little group.

'I wonder what the treasure is?' Jackie said.

Bradley shrugged. 'Maybe your grandad will know. I wish we could think of some way to get the map back.'

'We can't though,' Jackie said. 'Mike Dodger said such horrible things to us about the puppies. If we try to take it back, he might get the kennels closed down. It's not worth the risk.'

'Yeah, you're right, I suppose.' Bradley sighed. 'Come on, let's go and get an ice cream.'

The children walked off towards the

kiosk. Puzzle and Bounce followed, barking excitedly. Ice cream was even better than biscuits.

Einstein trotted after them but remained silent. He touched his smart bow-tie collar with his paw. Maybe there *was* a way they could beat Mike Dodger to the treasure after all.

# 5
# The Legend of The Hairy Mary

'Cowpat!'

Back at the lighthouse, the puppies scrambled up the wooden stairs to the den. Luckily they all remembered the password so no one got left out. Puzzle went first, then Bounce, then Einstein, who had to be lifted in again by his collar. 'Be careful with it this time,' he grumbled.

Puzzle rushed over to the window, grabbed the binoculars and looked out. 'There he is!' The diggercraft had reached the island. Puzzle watched as it crawled out of the water, up a ramp on to a jetty and turned back into a digger. Mike Dodger wobbled up the path to his house, clutching the biscuit tin, and disappeared inside.

'I think we should go to the island,' Bounce said, 'and snatch back the treasure map.'

'You're right,' said Puzzle. 'We found it, so we should have it.'

'If we can use the map to find the treasure, think how many dog biscuits the treasure could buy . . .' said Einstein, working it out in his head.

All three puppies were silent for a moment. They were all thinking about dog biscuits. Puzzle started to drool.

Bounce shook herself out of the daydream first. 'Right. So we need to get over to the island.'

'No, we don't,' Einstein said.

'But you just said we needed the map, and the map is on the island!'

'We do need the map, but I already have a copy,' Einstein said smugly.

Puzzle and Bounce looked at him in astonishment.

'Where is it then?' Puzzle asked, sniffing around him to look for it.

'It's not up my bottom,' Einstein told him crossly, 'or in my ears. It's in here.' He tapped the centre of the bow tie on the front of his collar. 'The reason I told you to be careful with it, Puzzle, is because this collar contains a hidden camera. Sometimes, when my owner is on an archaeological dig, she sends me into nooks and crannies with my collar-cam, so that she can watch the film on the computer afterwards and see if I've discovered anything interesting.' Einstein pressed on the centre of the bow tie with his paw. A tiny memory stick fell to the floor.

Puzzle looked at Einstein with surprise. 'So that's why you were fiddling with it on the beach! You were taking a photograph.'

'Precisely.'

'Now that,' Puzzle said, 'is a brilliant piece of detective work.'

'I know,' Einstein said proudly.

Puzzle switched the computer on at the plug on the wall. The computer screen lit up. Einstein wiggled the memory stick into the slot. Bounce bounced about, getting in the way. Then Puzzle gave Einstein a boost up on to the stool, while he and Bounce climbed on to the swivel chair. It was a bit of a squeeze with both of them,

especially as Bounce kept whizzing
the chair round and making Puzzle
dizzy, but eventually they settled down
to watch.

Einstein tapped some keys with his
front paws and a photo of a treasure
map appeared on the screen.

'That's where the lighthouse is,'
Bounce said, pushing Einstein out of the
way so she could get a better view. She
pointed at the map with a paw. 'That's
the causeway. Those are the rocks. And
that's the path down to Sandcliff Beach.
The X must be where the treasure is
buried.'

'Wait a minute!' Puzzle said.
'That oak tree is in
Mrs Bossy's garden!
In fact, I'd say the
X is pretty much
exactly where I dug
up her flower beds!'

'You're both wrong, my young friends,' Einstein said. 'You're looking at the treasure map upside down.'

'Excuse me, but I am not your "young" friend,' Puzzle said crossly. 'We're all puppies, so you can't be much older than me.'

'You're right, *technically*,' said Einstein. 'But I'm more grown-up because I'm cleverer than you.'

'No, you're not!' Puzzle said.

'Yes, I am.'

'No, you're not.'

'Yes, I am.'

'If you're so clever, how come you

can't even get up the stairs to the den?' Puzzle said.

'That's not an intelligence problem, it's because I'm very small,' said Einstein.

'All right then. If you've got such a small body, how can you have such a big brain?' Puzzle argued.

'Look,' Bounce said, 'we're all different sizes and we all have different *kinds* of intelligence. Einstein's good at taking photographs with his bow tie. I'm good at running, digging, climbing, bouncing, wagging my tail—'

'And I'm good at solving crimes,' Puzzle interrupted.

'No, you're not!' Einstein said.

'Yes, I am!'

'No, you're not!'

'Yes, I am!'

'Can we please get back to looking at the treasure map?' said Bounce.

They all focused on the screen again.

'Like I was saying,' Einstein began

again, 'we've been looking at the map upside down.' He tapped on the keyboard. The picture on the screen rotated 180 degrees.

'So the treasure's not in Mrs Bossy's garden after all . . .' Puzzle scratched his ear. He was still trying to figure the map out.

'So where is it?' Bounce asked.

'I've told you before – you need to think about the information.' Einstein grabbed the binoculars, climbed up on some books beside the computer and peered out the window. 'The rocks on the map are the ones over *there*.'

He pointed towards where Mike's house stood. 'Not the ones at the bottom of the lighthouse.'

'You mean the treasure's on the *island*?' Puzzle asked.

Einstein nodded.

'Oh no!' Bounce cried. 'If the treasure's on the island, that means Mike Dodger's bound to get to it before we do!'

'Not necessarily,' Einstein replied. 'He might make the same mistake as you did. He might think it's in Mrs Bossy's garden.'

'But what if he doesn't?' Bounce insisted. 'What if he works it out?'

'I've got a brilliant idea!' Puzzle said excitedly. 'Let's *trick* him into thinking that the treasure really *is* in Mrs Bossy's garden!'

'How do we do that?' Bounce asked.

'We make a false map, then sneak over to Mike Dodger's place and switch it for the real one. That way *we* can go after the treasure on the island, while Mike digs up Mrs Bossy's garden with his digger.'

'That *is* a good idea,' Einstein admitted.

Bounce wanted to start at once. 'Let's go!' she said. 'I'll race you across the causeway.'

'No, thanks,' Einstein said. 'For a start my legs are very short and you're bound to win so there's not much point.

And secondly, we have to draw a fake map first.'

'OK.' Bounce didn't mind. 'I'll do that.' She set about finding paper and coloured pens. She wanted to make it as good as possible to trick Mike.

'There is just one thing we haven't investigated,' Puzzle said, 'and that's what exactly we're looking for when we start digging for the treasure.'

'Let's see if we can find anything out on the internet,' Einstein said. He typed in 'Sandcliff' and 'treasure'. Several results came up on the screen, and Einstein clicked on one of them.

# The Legendary Treasure of the *Hairy Mary*

The *Hairy Mary* was a Tudor ship laden with treasure that ran aground off the treacherous coast of Sandcliff Bay.

Legend has it that before the ship finally sank, the surviving sailors rescued the treasure from the hold and rowed it to shore in lifeboats. There they hid it, meaning to return for it one day. They drew a map to show the exact spot and they put it in a biscuit tin to keep it dry. But in the chaos and confusion of the storm, the biscuit tin was lost.

Later that dreadful night, the sailors all drowned in the heavy seas. The treasure, so the story goes, remains hidden in a secret location somewhere near the Sandcliff Lighthouse.

Just at that moment the puppies heard Jackie calling them for dinner.

'Finished!' Bounce said, showing them the fake map. 'I've put a few extra details in to make Mike Dodger think it's definitely on the mainland.'

'Good work, Bounce,' Einstein said.

'We need a biscuit tin to put it in,' Bounce said. 'So we can just switch the tins when we get to the island. That old one that Mike took was jolly difficult to open. We might not have time to open it and put the map inside.'

Puzzle's eyes gleamed. 'I know!' he said. 'Let's eat all of Bounce's biscuits after tea,' he said. 'Then we can put it in there.'

'We can have a midnight feast!' Bounce cried.

For once all the puppies agreed that was the best idea they'd heard in ages.

Barking excitedly, they let themselves out of the den and shot off down the slide.

# 6
# Operation Biscuit Tin

The puppies guzzled their food as fast as possible so that they could get on with eating Bounce's biscuits afterwards. Meanwhile Jackie told Trevor all about Mike Dodger and the treasure map.

'Mike Dodger – I remember him from my schooldays,' said Trevor. 'He was always in trouble.' He shook his head. 'If that map is what I think it is, the treasure belongs in a museum, not in Mike Dodger's pocket. Everyone round here knows the story; it's part of our history.' He explained to Jackie about the legend of the *Hairy Mary*.

'I hadn't thought of that,' Bounce whispered, 'about the treasure belonging to a museum.'

'Trevor's right. The treasure isn't ours or Mike's to keep,' Einstein agreed. 'If we find it, we will have to return it. Then everyone will be able to learn about the past.'

'But we should be given some biscuits as a reward!' Puzzle said.

'Talking of biscuits, we need to get hold of Bounce's tin,' Einstein said. He nudged Jackie's leg with his nose. Bounce pawed Jackie's knee and Puzzle lay on the carpet in a heap, trying to show Jackie that he couldn't survive another second without a biscuit. Jackie laughed and stood up.

'I get the message. It's treat time, isn't it?'

She went to fetch the tin from the kitchen, gave the puppies a biscuit each, closed the lid and put the tin on the table. The puppies looked at each other. They didn't need to say anything because they were all thinking the same thing: Operation Biscuit Tin was going to plan! All they needed to do now was sneak down later and finish the biscuits, put the fake map in the tin and switch the biscuit tin with the one that Mike Dodger had.

Much later, a very long time after Jackie and Trevor had gone to bed, Bounce jumped out of her basket for the fiftieth time that evening. 'It must be midnight by now!' she said.

Einstein looked at the clock. He yawned. 'Yes it is, finally,' he said. Every time Bounce had bounced out of bed, he'd had to tell her the time.

'Great,' Puzzle said. 'Let's start the midnight feast! Who's going to get the biscuits?'

'I will,' said Bounce.

'I'll keep lookout,' Einstein offered.

'I'll doze until you get back,' Puzzle yawned.

Once they were all safely back in their room, the puppies leaped on the biscuits and tried to eat them as fast as possible.

Suddenly Einstein stopped chewing mid-biscuit. 'Hey, I just realized, we don't have to eat them all now. We could hide some for tomorrow or the next day.'

'We could . . .' said Puzzle, looking greedily at the biscuits. 'On the other hand, we could just finish them now. They're so delicious I don't think I can wait for tomorrow.'

'True,' said Einstein.

'You're right,' said Bounce.

So they gobbled them all up there
and then.

When they had finished, Puzzle
picked up the biscuit tin containing
the fake map and the three puppies
slid silently down to the bottom of the
lighthouse and sneaked out of the front
door. The night was clear and the moon

shone brightly. They were pleased to
see that the tide was still low enough
for them to walk across the causeway
to the island. Bounce started towards it.

'Wait!' Einstein whispered. 'We need
to make the tin look old first.'

Together the puppies rolled the tin
in the sand, wiped it with seaweed and
scratched it with shells. Soon it looked
as old as the tin from the *Hairy Mary*.

'Mike Dodger will never realize it's a different tin!' said Einstein, satisfied.

'Let's go,' said Bounce.

She began to cross the causeway. Puzzle followed, carrying the biscuit tin in his mouth. Einstein went last, checking behind him from time to time to make sure they hadn't been spotted.

After a while, they reached the island. The causeway ended near the bottom of a path that led up to Mike Dodger's house. The puppies clambered on to a platform and scampered up the path. They crept across the garden to the ground-floor window.

'Let me see!' Puzzle pushed in front.

'No, I want to!' Bounce pushed him back.

'So do I!' Einstein wriggled in between them.

'You're too short!' Puzzle said.

'So are you!' Einstein said. The window was so high even Puzzle couldn't see into it.

'This is hopeless!' Bounce said as they all pushed and shoved. 'Wait! I've got an idea. Einstein, you climb on to my back and I'll climb on to Puzzle, and then Einstein can see for all of us.'

'OK,' the other puppies agreed.

Puzzle lifted Einstein on to Bounce's
back. Then he planted his paws
squarely so she could climb on to his.

Einstein peered through the window.
'I can see Mike Dodger. He's still up!'

'But it's one o'clock in the morning!'
Bounce said. 'What's he doing?'

'He's brushing his hair,' Einstein
replied. 'But it's not on his head.'

'Where is it then?' asked Bounce.

'It's on a kind of plastic head on the
table.'

'That's a wig stand,' said Puzzle from
below. 'My owner's got one. We'd better
be careful. Mike Dodger might be
changing into disguise.'

'What are you talking about?'
Bounce said.

'My owner does undercover detective work,' Puzzle explained. 'Sometimes *he* has to get into disguise. I'm just saying, maybe that's what Mike's doing.'

'The wig isn't a disguise. He wears it because he's bald,' said Bounce.

'Maybe he wears it as a disguise *and* because he's bald,' said Puzzle.

'You don't know that for sure,' Einstein objected.

'And *you* don't understand the criminal mind,' Puzzle argued back.

'Oh shut up, you two!' Bounce hissed. 'Where's the biscuit tin?'

'On the table, next to the wig stand,'

Einstein whispered. He jumped down.

Bounce followed. 'What do we do now?' she asked.

'I know,' said Puzzle. 'I've seen this kind of thing on TV. We need to distract him so we can swap the biscuit tins. Einstein and I will hide behind that bush and start barking.' Puzzle pointed to a dense shrub beside the path. 'Mike will wonder what's going on and come out to look. Bounce, you hide over there.' He nodded towards a large plant pot next to the front door. 'When he comes out, you scoot into the house and swap the tins. Any questions?'

Bounce and Einstein shook their heads. Puzzle gave Bounce the biscuit tin. 'Positions everyone,' he said.

'I wish you'd stop showing off,' Einstein grumbled. 'It's not a detective show.'

'It's more like one of my owner's films!' Bounce said happily. 'I've always wanted to be a stunt puppy.'

'Well, whatever it is, someone's got to be in charge of operations,' Puzzle said. 'And that's me.'

'Unfortunately,' Einstein muttered under his breath.

The puppies went into action. Puzzle and Einstein hid behind the bush.

'Woof, woof, woof, woof!' they barked.

The front door opened. Mike Dodger came out of the house. He looked around crossly.

'Woof, woof, woof, woof!'

Cursing to himself, Mike Dodger struggled down the path in his platform shoes. 'Who's there?' he called.

Bounce dashed into the house.

'Keep barking!' Einstein said. 'We don't want him to go back into the house while Bounce is in there.'

'Woof, woof, woof, woof!' Puzzle obliged. He liked barking.

'Get off my property!' Mike shouted.

'Woof, woof, woof, woof!'

There was a crash from inside the
house. Mike Dodger spun round.

'Oh no!' Einstein said. 'He's going back in.'

'Woof, woof, woof, woof!' The two puppies kept barking, but Mike paid them no more attention. He strode back inside the house and slammed the door shut.

'Bounce will have to use all her intelligence if she is to outsmart Mike Dodger now,' Puzzle said.

'Well then, we're doomed,' Einstein sighed.

Meanwhile, inside the house, Bounce was looking for a place to hide. When she had switched the biscuit tins, she had accidentally knocked the wig stand off the table. That's what had made the crashing noise.

There were lots of sensible places to hide, like under the chair or behind the sofa, but Bounce panicked. As soon as she heard Mike come back in the front door, she jumped up on to the table where the wig stand had been, put the wig on her head and sat on the old biscuit tin. As soon as she had done this, she realized what a stupid idea it was. Surely Mike would notice that his wig was now being worn by a dog?

Mike came into the room.

'Who's there?' he said.

He looked all around.

But Bounce was in luck. Maybe it
was because in the dim light the black
wig looked the same colour as the
dark patches on Bounce's coat or
more likely because he was thinking
about what he was going to buy with

the treasure, but Mike didn't seem to notice her.

'Must have been the wind,' he muttered. He picked up the wig, collected the fake biscuit tin and went to bed.

# 7
# Dodging Dodger

Bounce crept to the front door and opened it. She tiptoed out and closed it behind her without a sound. Then she bounced down the path, the biscuit tin between her teeth, to where Einstein and Puzzle were waiting. She placed the tin on the ground.

'You did it!' Einstein said, astonished. 'You escaped!'

'With the right biscuit tin,' Bounce said proudly. She quickly explained how she'd put the wig on her head and how Mike Dodger had thought she was a wig stand. 'Honestly, I don't know how he didn't see me!' she said.

'That's because he wasn't *expecting* to see you,' Puzzle said. 'It's a trick that criminals use: if they want to hide something, they put it in an obvious place, where the detective won't think of looking.'

'Oh,' said Bounce. 'That's a good idea. I'll try that next time I get a bone.' She led off back down the path towards the causeway. Then she stopped. 'Is it just me, or has someone hidden the path? It doesn't seem to be there any more!'

Einstein and Puzzle joined her at the bottom of the path. The puppies looked hard. Where an hour earlier there had been a path through the sea, now there was only sea.

'She's right.' Puzzle frowned. 'It's gone.'

'Someone must have stolen it!' Bounce said indignantly.

'When we weren't looking!' Puzzle agreed crossly. 'This place is full of criminals! I'll bet it was that lollipop lady I saw in the village when we first arrived.'

'You're both wrong,' Einstein said. 'Again! No one's stolen it. There's a perfectly good scientific reason why the causeway has disappeared.'

'What?' Puzzle asked suspiciously.

'When we came to the island the sea was at low tide. Now the tide's coming in and the sea has covered the causeway,' Einstein explained. 'That's why it's invisible.'

'You mean we're stuck?' Bounce said. 'But what about Jackie? And Trevor? And our owners? They'll be really sad if

we never come back.'
She slumped down on
the rock and put her
paws over her eyes.
'I don't want to be
stuck here forever!'

'We won't be stuck here forever,'
Einstein explained. 'We can cross
the causeway at the next low tide
which, by my reckoning, will be in
approximately six hours from now.'

'Six hours!' Bounce sobbed. 'That's
like a lifetime!'

'Only if you're a mayfly,' Einstein
said patiently. 'Not if you're a dog.'

'Jackie will be worried about us,' Bounce persisted.

'And we need to show her the map,' Puzzle added, 'so that she and Bradley can come back here with us and help us find the treasure while Mike's digging up Mrs Bossy's garden.'

'Then we must think of another way to get back,' Einstein said.

'We could swim!' Bounce cried. 'I love swimming! And it's not that far. I know, let's have a doggy-paddle race.'

'No, thanks,' said Einstein. 'For a start, you'd win because your legs are much longer than mine. And for a second, I'd drown because I don't know how to swim.'

'I could teach you,' Bounce offered.

Einstein shook his head firmly. 'We haven't got time for that,' he said.

'I know!' Puzzle said. 'We can get back to the mainland in the diggercraft.'

He bounded along the platform towards the digger. Einstein trotted after him. Bounce bounced. 'But that's stealing,' she panted.

'Technically it's only borrowing, if we intend to return it,' Einstein corrected her.

'But how does it work?' Bounce asked.

'There's only one way to find out,' said Puzzle. He lifted Einstein into the cab. Bounce leaped up after him. The three puppies sat in a line on the cab seat.

'It seems pretty straightforward,' Puzzle said, looking at the instrument panel. 'Like driving a car, only it's a diggercraft.'

'Wow! You know how to drive a car?' Bounce exclaimed.

'Well, not really,' Puzzle admitted, 'but my owner lets me sit on his knee sometimes when he's parking.'

'That's not exactly driving,' Einstein muttered. He and Bounce looked at each other doubtfully.

'It can't be that difficult.' Puzzle pressed the ignition. The diggercraft engine began to chug. With one front

paw he slid the gear stick to DRIVE.
Then he released the handbrake. The
diggercraft trundled towards the water.

Bounce peered out of the cab. 'We're
sinking,' she said.

'Help!' Einstein said. 'You forgot to
press the FLOAT button.'

Puzzle punched FLOAT. Just in time, the inflatable rubber cushion started to fill with air. Very soon the diggercraft was heading across the water, away from the island and towards the lighthouse.

'Hooray!' Bounce cried. 'We did it!'

'Not quite.' Einstein peered out into the darkness. 'You've forgotten something – the rocks near the lighthouse.'

'But I thought ships had equipment to tell them where the rocks are.' Bounce frowned. 'You said that's why the lighthouse isn't needed any more.'

'Ships do,' Einstein said gravely, 'but this diggercraft doesn't, does it, Puzzle?'

'No.' Puzzle shook his head. 'Only headlights.' He switched them on. It helped a bit to see where they were going.

'We can see better now,' said Bounce.

'Yes, but these headlights aren't strong enough. We won't see the rocks until it's too late!' Einstein said.

'There's only one thing for it then,' Bounce said bravely. 'I'll swim back to the lighthouse and switch on the light.'

'It's too dangerous,' Einstein said.

'Nothing's too dangerous for me!' Bounce said. 'I'll swim to the beach, run back to the lighthouse, nip up to the control room, switch on the light and wait for you in the den.'

'But—'

'We've got no choice, Einstein,' Puzzle said. 'Not if you can't swim. No one's blaming you or anything,' he added hastily. Even Puzzle could see that Einstein looked miserable.

'I can't help being small,' Einstein said.

'Of course you can't!' Bounce said cheerfully. 'Just like I can't help being bouncy. Now, how do I turn on the light?'

'You need to press the big red switch on the control panel,' Einstein told her.

'Roger,' Bounce said.

'My name's not Roger,' Einstein said. 'It's Einstein.'

'I know. It's just what they say in adventure movies when someone gets an order!' Bounce said. She opened the window of the cab.

'Be careful,' said Puzzle. He licked her nose affectionately.

'I will.' Bounce slipped out of the cab into the water. Before long she was out of view of the headlights, moving at a swift doggy-paddle towards the beach.

'We'd better cut the engine and wait until she turns on the light.' Puzzle put the diggercraft in NEUTRAL and they drifted with the waves. The two puppies sat in silence.

Puzzle tried to think of something to do to make the time go faster. 'Would you like to play I Spy?' he suggested.

'I don't think that would work,' Einstein replied, 'as we can't see anything.'

They waited in silence for what
seemed like ages.

Suddenly a beam
of strong light
flooded the sea.

'She's done it!'
Einstein cried.

'Just in time.' Puzzle pointed to their right. The diggercraft was only metres away from the rocks. They had nearly drifted on to them without realizing.

Puzzle put the gear stick into DRIVE and hit the accelerator. They chugged away from the rocks and towards the beach. Very soon the diggercraft crawled out of the water and on to the sand.

'Phew!' Puzzle said. 'That was close.' He looked at Einstein. The little dachshund's teeth were chattering. 'Are you all right?'

'I'm cold,' Einstein shivered, 'and very

tired. I don't know if I can make it all the way back up to the lighthouse.' He sighed. 'Sometimes it's hard being a small dog with a big brain.'

'I can see that,' Puzzle said kindly. 'But don't worry – on this occasion a *big* dog with an even bigger brain is going to help you out.'

'Your brain's not bigger than mine,' Einstein said.

'It must be, because my head's bigger,' Puzzle reasoned. 'Now, do you want a lift or not?'

Einstein nodded. He was too tired to argue.

'Get on my back.' Puzzle crouched down on the sand while Einstein climbed up. 'Hold on to my ears,' Puzzle said. Once he was sure Einstein wouldn't fall off, he made his way quickly back to the lighthouse to join Bounce.

# 8
# Mrs Bossy's Garden

**BASH! BASH! BASH!**

Early next morning the puppies were woken up by a loud banging at the front door of the lighthouse.

'Who's that?' Einstein grumbled.

'Let's go and find out.' Bounce led the way down the slide.

But when they got to the bottom and saw who it was, the three puppies quickly hid behind a sofa.

It was Mike Dodger! He was standing on the doorstep talking angrily to Jackie and Trevor.

'I just had a call from the coastguard,' he shouted. 'Apparently my diggercraft's on Sandcliff Beach and I want to know how it got there!'

'Calm down, Mike,' Trevor said. 'Keep your hair on. We don't know anything about your diggercraft.'

'I reckon *she* does –' Mike jabbed a finger at Jackie – 'and that mate of hers who was at the sandcastle competition yesterday!'

'No, I don't!' Jackie cried. 'Honestly, Grandad. I didn't take it!'

Just then Bradley turned up on his bike. When he saw Mike Dodger his face fell. 'Is everything OK?' he asked Jackie.

'Mike thinks you and Jackie took his diggercraft,' Trevor explained.

'How could we?' Bradley looked astonished. 'We don't know how to drive.'

'Well, I heard dogs outside my house last night,' Mike grumbled. 'Maybe you brought them over to make trouble.'

'It couldn't have been the puppies,' Jackie shot back. 'They were asleep upstairs here.'

'Well, someone took my diggercraft! So you'd better watch it! And *you'd* better keep an eye on those kids, Trevor. And those mangy dogs. You don't want your kennels to be closed down, do you?'

'Now hang on a minute . . .' Trevor protested.

'I haven't got time to hang on, Trev.

I've got treasure to dig up. I'm going to be on TV.'

'That treasure doesn't belong to you, Mike—' Trevor began.

'Finders keepers,' Mike said, 'losers weepers. Too bad you didn't find the treasure map yourself, Trev.'

'But *we* did!' Jackie cried. 'At least, the puppies did!'

'They'll enjoy watching me dig it up then.' Mike Dodger turned and lurched off down the cliff path in his platform shoes.

The puppies had been listening in silence.

'I feel bad that the kids got accused of taking the digger,' Bounce whispered.

'Me too,' said Puzzle, 'but we can't exactly tell them it was us, can we?'

'They should teach kids barking at school,' said Einstein.

'Well, we might as well watch, I suppose,' Trevor said with a sigh. 'See what Mike finds.' He switched on the TV.

The puppies crept out from behind the sofa. They lay on the rug in front of the humans.

It didn't take Mike Dodger long to make it to the beach. Very soon the camera showed him driving his

diggercraft along the sand past a crowd
of onlookers and through the neat little
front garden of a tidy yellow cottage.
An old woman was standing on the
garden path, looking very cross.

'That's Gran,' said Bradley. 'Oh my
goodness,' he gasped. 'Mike Dodger's
digging up her garden. Gran will be
furious.'

'She's always furious,' Trevor chuckled. 'She has been since she was a kid. I know because I was at school with her. Mind you,' he said seriously, 'I'd be furious if someone dug up my front garden!'

'Should we try to stop him?' Jackie asked Bradley.

'It's too late,' said Bradley, watching the digger's huge scoop cut deeper and deeper into the rich soil.

'I forgot that Mrs Bossy was Bradley's gran,' said Bounce quietly. 'I hope he's not cross if he ever finds out it was because of us that Mike dug up her garden.'

'He won't be cross if he realizes *why* we did it. Motive is very important in detective work,' said Puzzle.

'You are both missing one vital point,' said Einstein. 'He won't find out. I mean, who's going to ever suspect that a *dog* drew a map?!'

They were interrupted by the TV interviewer shouting at Mike Dodger over the noise of the digger: 'Are you sure the treasure is there? It's a long way down if it is.'

'Of course I'm sure. It's marked on the map!' Mike shouted back as he picked up the fake map and pointed with his muddy finger to the cross that Bounce had drawn. Mrs Bossy stuck her face right up close to the camera. The puppies could see the bristles on her chin. 'There's no treasure here,' she said. 'Leave my garden alone!'

Just then they all heard the sound of the scoop hitting something hard. Mike Dodger's face broke into a big smile. The puppies pricked up their ears.

'What could that be?' said Bounce.

'It can't be the *Hairy Mary* treasure,' replied Einstein. 'That's on the island.'

'So what is it then?' Puzzle asked.

Mike Dodger jumped down from the cab, bent over and brushed away the earth with his hand. Then he grabbed something and lifted it up!

It was an old loo seat.

The children giggled.

'Now what's he doing?' Bounce whispered.

Mike Dodger didn't seem to believe that there wasn't any treasure in Mrs Bossy's garden. He moved from the flower beds to the lawn and started digging up the grass.

'Look at this!' He held up a pair of rusty toenail clippers and a plastic baby spoon for the TV camera to film.

The camera zoomed in on the spoon. 'You sure that's from the *Hairy Mary*?' the TV presenter said. 'I didn't think they had plastic spoons in those days.'

'Course they did,' Mike said. 'I reckon it's priceless.'

'Get off my lawn!' Mrs Bossy screeched. 'Or I'll have you arrested. You can't go round digging up people's gardens without their permission.'

Just then the police arrived on the scene. There was pandemonium as Mike tried to run away. His wig fell off. He grimaced, clutched his bald head, then bent down to retrieve the wig but he tripped over his platform shoes, landing face down in something nasty near to where he'd been digging.

'Dog poo!' Mrs Bossy screamed. 'In my beautiful garden!'

'Whoops.' Puzzle looked embarrassed. 'That might have been me.'

The police had handcuffed Mike Dodger and were leading him away.

'Serves him right!' Trevor got up and went to make a cup of coffee.

'Now's our chance to get the treasure,' Puzzle whispered.

'We'll need Jackie's help,' Einstein said.

'I'll go and get the biscuit tin.' Bounce raced upstairs and returned with the tin in her mouth. She dropped it at Jackie's feet and nudged it towards her.

'It's not treat time,' Jackie said, picking up the tin. She looked at it. 'Wait a minute – this isn't Bounce's biscuit tin.'

'Woof, woof, woof, woof!' the dogs barked, trying to make her understand.

Jackie showed the tin to Bradley.

'It's the one Bounce found on the beach yesterday,' he said, examining it carefully. 'The one that Mike Dodger stole. The one with the treasure map in it.' His voice was becoming more excited.

'But how did it end up here?' Jackie said.

'Woof, woof, woof, woof!' the puppies barked more loudly.

Bradley looked at them. 'Didn't Mike say something about hearing dogs outside his house last night?' he said slowly.

'But you don't think the puppies took it, do you?'

'Woof, woof, woof! Woof, woof, woof!'

'Actually, yes I do.' Bradley grinned. 'That's what they're trying to tell us. Isn't it, puppies?'

# 9
# Treasure Dogs

'Woof, woof, woof, woof.' The puppies jumped about, barking and licking Bradley's hand.

'They must have gone across to the island and taken it!' he said.

'But you don't think *they* drove the diggercraft back?' Jackie asked.

'No, of course not!' Bradley laughed. 'Someone else must have taken that for a joke! Puppies can't drive. They must have gone across the causeway at low tide, sneaked into the house and grabbed the tin.' He opened the tin and took out the real treasure map.

Jackie's face lit up in a broad smile. 'I always knew dogs were just as intelligent as humans!' She laughed. 'Well done, puppies!' She gave them each a hug.

'I'm so pleased they've worked out it was us that got the tin from the *Hairy Mary* back!' said Bounce.

'And I'm so pleased they *haven't* worked out that we drew a fake map and planted it at Mike's house in Bounce's bashed-up biscuit tin!' said Einstein. 'They might be upset if they realized we're even *more* intelligent than they are!'

'They're not very good at being detectives,' Puzzle remarked.

Jackie and Bradley were looking closely at the map.

'So, if the treasure's not in your gran's garden, where is it?' Jackie asked him.

'Well,' said Bradley, turning the map around like the puppies had done on the computer, 'maybe Mike read the map the wrong way up.'

The two children pored over the map. 'I think you might be right,' said Jackie. 'Look. That's the causeway. And those are the rocks!'

'Yes!' Bradley pointed to the X triumphantly. 'The treasure's on the island!' He grinned. 'Mike Dodger's going to have a fit when he finds out it was right under his nose all along. Only by the time he does, we'll have dug it up and taken it to the local museum so that everyone can enjoy it.'

'Let's go and find it then –' Jackie pulled on her jumper – 'while Mike Dodger's at the police station.'

Bradley looked out of the window. 'Just one problem, Jackie,' he said. 'We'd better not go across the causeway.

We might not be able to get back because of the tide.'

Jackie grinned at him. 'Who said anything about going across the causeway?' she said. 'We'll take Grandad's boat. He said I could borrow it whenever I wanted.'

She grabbed a life jacket and chucked another at Bradley. He put the map back in the tin and put the tin under his arm. They were ready to go!

'Phew! That was hard work!' Bounce said a few minutes later as the puppies jumped into the little dinghy after the children. The boat sped away from the beach. 'I didn't think we'd ever make them understand.'

'My throat's sore from barking,' Einstein grumbled.

'Puzzle's right. The kids aren't very good at being detectives.' Bounce frowned. 'I mean, they didn't have a clue about you two driving the diggercraft or me swimming back and turning the light on.'

'That's why they need us,' Einstein said. 'A dog is man's best friend.'

'Jackie's not a man,' Puzzle objected, 'nor is Bradley. He's a boy.'

'It's a saying,' Einstein explained. 'It just means humans rely on dogs to look after them. Humans think it's the other way round, but obviously it isn't. They wouldn't be able to do anything without dogs. Trust me – we do all the work.'

'You haven't done anything. You've

just talked,' Puzzle muttered under his breath.

'I don't do any work,' Bounce said. 'I don't do anything at all except bounce.'

'Well, I do,' Einstein said crossly. 'I'm a sniffer dog. I find things. And there are lots of other working dogs, such as guide dogs, police dogs, rescue dogs . . .'

'Detective dogs,' Puzzle said, remembering he was one.

Einstein nodded. 'Sled dogs, guard dogs, hearing dogs . . . er . . .'

'Treasure dogs,' Bounce cried, 'like us!'

'Treasure dogs!' Einstein looked

pleased. 'Well done, Bounce, you're beginning to use your brain at last. I'm glad my influence is rubbing off on you.'

'The only thing that's rubbed off from you on to me is a small flea,' said Bounce.

For once Einstein had nothing to say except, 'Sorry about that.'

They were approaching the island. Jackie brought them expertly in to land, coming in slow alongside the jetty. Bradley jumped out and tied the boat to a mooring post with a rope. Bounce and Puzzle leaped after him. Einstein waited for Jackie. He didn't want to fall down the gap between the boat and the jetty! She picked him up and stepped carefully on to the wooden platform. 'There you go,' she said, putting him down.

Einstein licked her ankle gratefully.

Bradley removed the map from the biscuit tin, where he had kept it safe from the sea spray. He unfolded it and held it up so that Jackie could see it too.

'We follow the path along the shore,' Bradley said, 'until we get to a big oak tree.'

Bounce raced off. 'Woof, woof, woof, woof!'

The others panted along behind her. They clambered up the rocks on to the path that led away from Mike's house. Gradually the path dropped down towards a sandy beach. In front of them was the oak. Dappled sunlight filtered through its great branches.

'The treasure's there,' Bradley said, 'under the oak tree. That's what the map says. X marks the spot.'

'But we'll never be able to dig under that!' said Jackie, looking at the huge tree. The ground around it was hard and twisted with roots where the oak had grown over the hundreds of years since the sailors came. If it had been big then, it was massive now. 'We'd need the diggercraft!' Her face creased in disappointment.

'Poor Jackie,' Bounce whispered. 'I wish there was something we could do to help.'

'There is,' Einstein said. 'There might be another way to get to the treasure.'

'How?' asked Puzzle.

'The oak is on the edge of the bank,' Einstein said.

'So?' asked Bounce.

'The bank has fallen away into the sea.'

Puzzle and Bounce looked past the trunk. On the other side of the oak tree the bank fell away sharply to the beach.

'So?' asked Puzzle.

'The land beneath the oak has been washed away by the sea,' Einstein explained.

'You mean there might be a cave underneath?' Puzzle said excitedly.

'Exactly.' Einstein nodded.

Puzzle led the way to the edge of the bank. The roots of the great tree had made natural steps in the soil, like a ladder. He bounded down with Bounce.

Einstein followed carefully, letting himself down backward.

The three dogs could hear the children's voices behind them.

'What are the puppies doing?' Jackie was saying.

'I don't know,' Bradley replied. 'Let's go and see.'

The puppies had reached the beach. They sat in a line, looking towards the bank, wagging their tails.

Sure enough, beneath
the great oak tree was the
opening to a cave.

Bradley and Jackie climbed down after them.

'Oh, you clever things!' Jackie exclaimed.

'I never thought of that!' Bradley laughed.

'I told you people need dogs,' Einstein said.

'They never would have found the cave without our help,' agreed Puzzle.

'What do you mean, *our* help?! It was my idea,' Einstein said indignantly.

'No, it wasn't!'

'Yes, it was!'

'No, it wasn't!'

'Never mind that,' Bounce said. 'Who's going first?'

'I am,' Puzzle said. 'I'm the biggest.'

'But I want to,' Bounce said. 'I'm the bounciest.'

'But you don't know where you're going,' Puzzle said.

'Neither do you!'

'Well, I do,' Einstein said firmly. 'It's like on a dig. Follow me!'

# 10
# See You
# Next Year

Einstein walked forward and led the
way into the cave, his head held high,
the tip of his nose twitching. The other
two puppies and the children followed.
The children had to crouch down so
they didn't bump their heads.

They were right under the big oak
tree now. Although it was dark in the
cave, they could make out the thick

roots making shapes in the roof. As their
eyes got used to the darkness they saw
that there were several paths leading off
the cave.

'Now what?' said Puzzle. 'Which one
do we take?'

Einstein moved forward, picking the
left-hand path.

'He seems to know the way,' said
Bounce.

'Maybe he's secretly so old he was
around when they buried the treasure,'
said Puzzle to Bounce quietly.

'I heard that,' Einstein said. 'Actually,
it's because I'm used to doing this with
my owner. Which reminds me, I need to
switch on my live-streaming device.'

'What's that?' asked Bounce.

'The camera in my collar is connected
to the internet,' Einstein explained,
'so that when I'm investigating
archaeological remains I can stream the
pictures straight on to the web. That way

everyone gets to see what I discover while I'm discovering it. It makes it more exciting.'

'What's he talking about?' Bounce asked Puzzle.

'No idea,' Puzzle replied. 'Sounds good though.'

A little further Einstein stopped and barked.

'Einstein's found something!' Bradley shouted.

Jackie and Bradley moved quickly ahead to see. When they reached Einstein, they saw that the path ended in a second, smaller cave. Against the wall

of the cave was
a pile of rocks
and sticks. Einstein
stood beside it,
barking loudly.

'This is it!' Einstein
said to his puppy friends.
'It's under here.'

'How do you know?' Puzzle
challenged him.

'Because I've got an incredible sense
of smell,' Einstein said. 'Beneath this pile
lies a wooden treasure chest from the
year 1545. In it is the treasure from the
*Hairy Mary.*'

'Let's dig it out!' Bounce cried.

Einstein stood back.

'Aren't you going to help?' Puzzle asked.

'No. I'm doing the filming,' said Einstein. 'I don't want to break my collar-cam. Anyway, you're bigger than me.'

Bounce and Puzzle knew there was no point arguing with Einstein about his collar-cam, so they dug in with their paws and got on with the work. The kids quickly got the idea and joined in.

'It must be under there,' Jackie said. She and Bradley helped lift the bigger rocks away.

They were a good team and only minutes later the dark old wood of the Tudor treasure chest was revealed.

'This is it!' Jackie breathed. 'The *Hairy Mary* treasure.' She lifted the lid. It opened with a creak.

The puppies looked inside the chest in amazement. There were heaps of gold coins, piles of rubies and pearls and a diamond-encrusted skull and crossbones. The treasure shone and twinkled. The children and the puppies were silent. They were all astounded.

'That would buy an awful lot of biscuits,' said Bounce quietly.

'Shh,' said Einstein. 'It's for everyone, remember?'

'But they *will* give us a couple, won't they, after all we've done?' said Puzzle.

Bradley was the first of the children to speak. 'We've got to get this out of here,' he said.

'Thanks for offering!' said a sharp voice behind them. 'You can carry it back to the house for me.'

It was Mike Dodger. There was mud in his wig and one of Mrs Bossy's flowers sticking out of his ear.

'It doesn't belong to you,' Jackie said.

'Yes, it does!' Mike roared. 'One of my ancestors was on the *Hairy Mary*!'

'What was his name?' Jackie asked suspiciously.

'Sir Francis Dodger,' Mike said.

'I don't believe you,' Bradley said.

'It doesn't matter anyway,' Mike snarled. 'That treasure's mine. It's on the island, and I've lived here all my life.'

'That's not true either!' said Bradley. 'Gran told me you moved down here when you were three!'

'That's a lie!' said Mike savagely. 'I was four! Now give me the treasure.' He lunged forward. The children took a step backward.

'Don't worry, I'm getting all this on camera,' said Einstein. 'It can be used against him in court.'

'Never mind court,' Puzzle said.
'We've got to arrest him first.'

'Never mind arresting him,' said
Bounce, 'let's take him out.' Without
another word she leaped into the air
and snatched Mike's wig in her mouth.

'Catch!' She threw it to Puzzle.
Puzzle put it on and bounded around
the cave.

'Give that back, you mangy mutt!'
Mike Dodger made a grab for his
wig but he couldn't see very well in
the dark cave. By mistake he grabbed
Einstein and put him on his head
instead.

Mike's bald head was slippery and Einstein scrabbled to keep a hold. His bottom kept sliding off. He grabbed Mike's ears with his claws.

Mike screamed. 'Aarrrrgghhhh! There's a dog on my head!'

Jackie and Bradley started to giggle.

Mike staggered about.

Jackie saw an opportunity. She slid the biscuit tin across the floor towards Mike's feet. It landed just in front of him. Mike took a step forward on his platform shoes and tripped on the tin.

'WHOOOOAAAA!' he cried.

Einstein flew off Mike's head.

'I've got him!' Bradley held out his arms and Einstein landed safely.

Mike shot forward and sprawled on to the treasure chest – which was still open.

'Quick! Help me close the lid!' Bounce yelled. She and Puzzle lifted the heavy lid of the chest with their front paws and slammed it down on top of Mike Dodger so that only his platform shoes stuck out at the end.

A round of applause erupted around the cave.

The children and the puppies turned in surprise.

A group of people had come into the cave holding torches. Trevor was at the front.

'Well done, kids!' Trevor congratulated them. 'We thought you might need a hand. But you seem to have managed fine on your own.'

'What are you doing here, Grandad?' asked Jackie. 'How did you find us?'

'Einstein's owner rang me and told me to watch you on the computer. You were being streamed on the internet! Apparently Einstein has a camera in his collar.'

'Wow!' said Jackie. 'So they didn't just help us find the treasure, they managed to film at the same time! Clever puppies!'

She gave each one of them a huge hug.

Five days later, on a sunny afternoon, a large crowd stood outside the town museum. A brass band played, and

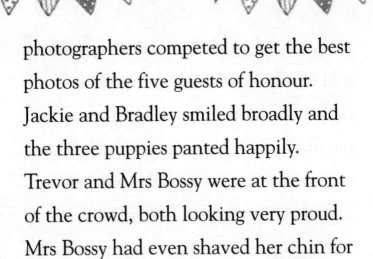

photographers competed to get the best
photos of the five guests of honour.
Jackie and Bradley smiled broadly and
the three puppies panted happily.
Trevor and Mrs Bossy were at the front
of the crowd, both looking very proud.
Mrs Bossy had even shaved her chin for
the occasion. Then the mayor came

forward and pinned medals on Jackie's and Bradley's T-shirts, and one on each of the three puppies' collars. The puppies were a given a large sack of dog biscuits each, which made them even happier. They wagged their tails.

'Thank you,' Einstein barked politely.

'Finally, some more biscuits!' Puzzle drooled. 'Do you think anyone would mind if we ate them now?'

'I don't care if they mind. I'm starving,' said Bounce.

The puppies tore into the sacks.

The crowd clapped and cheered.

After the ceremony the puppies wandered back to the lighthouse along the beach with the children. They walked past Mrs Bossy's garden, where Mike Dodger was planting new flowers to replace the ones he had dug up. This was not because he had turned into a nice, kind person. It was because the police had told him to do it to make up for the ones he had destroyed.

'I don't want this holiday to end. I want to stay here forever,' Bounce said with a sigh.

'But don't you want to see your owner again?' asked Puzzle.

'Yes, I really miss her! Maybe I do want to go home!' said Bounce. 'I can't make my mind up.'

'Maybe we can keep in touch and tell each other what we've been doing,' said Puzzle.

Bounce was so excited about this idea that she ran around in circles a few times. Then she stopped dead still. 'But how can we?' she asked the others.

'We could text . . .' said Einstein.

'We could email . . .' said Puzzle.

'We could blog . . .'

'We could chat online . . .'

'We could message . . .'

'Or we could meet in the park!' said Bounce. 'If we went to the same park.'

'Or we could just see each other back here next holiday,' said Einstein.

'That's a great idea!' barked Bounce.

'I agree,' said Puzzle, 'but how will we make sure our owners send us here at the same time?'

'I'll sort that out,' said Einstein. 'Don't forget, I'm the cleverest.'

'No, you're not!'

'Yes, I am!'

'No, you're not!'

Bounce sighed. 'If you two don't shut up, I'll eat all your biscuits as well as mine.'

The other two went quiet.

'That's better,' said Bounce. 'Now,' she said happily, 'when's our next midnight feast?'

# Watch out!

The puppies will be back very soon
in an all-new adventure.

# Puppies
# Online

# Puffin
# Patrol

Coming spring 2015

# Quiz Time With Einstein!

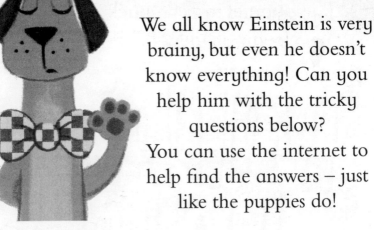

We all know Einstein is very brainy, but even he doesn't know everything! Can you help him with the tricky questions below?

You can use the internet to help find the answers – just like the puppies do!

**1** Puppies are good at lots of things. But what are they *really* good at?

ⓐ Knitting
ⓑ Smelling things
ⓒ Playing the piano

**2** What is the name of the very tall building that shows sailors the way home?

ⓐ The Pyramids
ⓑ Big Ben
ⓒ Lighthouse

**3** Einstein's owner's job involves digging underground to find out about people who lived long ago. But what is this job called?

(a) Stunt-woman
(b) Ice-cream van driver
(c) Archaeologist

**4** What do the pups call the secret snack that they eat in the middle of the night?

(a) Nighttime Nibbles
(b) Midnight Feast
(c) Daytime Biscuit

**5** What are dogs often told to do by humans?

(a) Make coffee
(b) Sit
(c) Help finish the crossword

*Answers on page 206*

# Puzzle's Puzzle!

Puzzle, as we all know, loves nothing more than puzzles. But he's also quite lazy, so he'd love if you could help him with this word search:

**DETECTIVE**
**CLUE**
**MYSTERY**
**CRIMINAL**
**TREASURE**

```
C D S O T F S J G C
T R E A S U R E D B
F Y I T D U Q Q Z Y
Y R P M E V I L R P
Z C O A I C Y E R U
I Q D Y N N T W H E
P I D U M S A I U W
G H X G Y R X L V K
S B A M K N C U G E
W E V Q O I N M S R
```

# Bounce Gets Lost!

Bounce doesn't like puzzles at all – she prefers to bounce around outdoors! But sometimes, she gets lost. Can you help her find the way back to the lighthouse?

*Answers on page 206*

GUINEA PIGS ONLINE
VIKING VICTORY
'HAY-LARIOUS!' Micespace.com
JENNIFER GRAY & AMANDA SWIFT

WITH BONUS ACTIVITIES!
GUINEA PIGS ONLINE
CHRISTMAS QUEST
JENNIFER GRAY & AMANDA SWIFT

With BONUS ACTIVITIES!
GUINEA PIGS ONLINE
BUNNY TROUBLE
'EGG-CELLENT!' Micespace.com
JENNIFER GRAY & AMANDA SWIFT

Read an extract from the first book in the brilliant GUINEA PIGS ONLINE series!

# 1

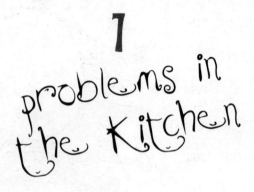

problems in the Kitchen

London is home to thousands and thousands of guinea pigs.

Fuzzy and Coco were two of them. They lived in a very nice terraced house in Strawberry Park – number 7, Middleton Crescent – with their owners, Mr Ben and Mrs

Henrietta Bliss. Fuzzy
was Ben's; Coco
belonged to
Henrietta.

Ben Bliss ran
the Strawberry
Park Animal
Rescue Centre.
When Ben first
found Fuzzy, lying
on his back with his
legs in the air in a rusty old hutch at
the bottom of the garden of an empty
house, Ben rushed him straight to the
nearest vet, who just happened to be

Henrietta. Once they were sure that Fuzzy would be all right, Ben and Henrietta promptly fell in love over the operating table.

Afterwards, Ben decided to keep Fuzzy, who was brown and round with a white crest on his forehead, because he brought him luck. 'A wife and a pet,' Ben would joke, 'all in one afternoon.'

Actually it turned out to be a wife and *two* pets because, by a strange coincidence, Henrietta had mysteriously found a dazed-looking Coco at the bottom of her handbag only the week before and, when her real owner didn't come forward, decided to keep her too.

When the Blisses got married, Fuzzy and Coco were very pleased. Guinea pigs squeak when they are happy, and Fuzzy and Coco squeaked a great deal. As everyone knows, guinea pigs like company.

*For longer extracts, games and lots more,*
*go to guineapigsonline.co.uk*

# Answers

## Quiz Time with Einstein!

1(b)  2(c)  3(c)  4(b)  5(b)

## Puzzle's Puzzle!

## Bounce Gets Lost!

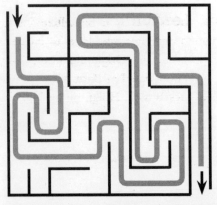

# About the authors and illustrator

**Jennifer Gray** loves writing about animals and imagining what sort of adventures they get up to when humans aren't looking. Her other books include a comedy series starring Atticus Claw, the world's greatest cat burglar, the first of which – *Atticus Claw Breaks the Law* – won the 2014 Red House Book Award in the Younger Readers category. Jennifer lives in central London and Scotland with her husband, four children and her pampered and overfed cat, Henry.

**Amanda Swift** first worked as an actress, once appearing in a commercial for Angel Delight! She has written several books for children, including *The Boys' Club* and *Anna/Bella*. She lives in south-east London with her translator husband and two teenage sons.

**Steven Lenton** is a bestselling illustrator and award-winning animator who loves to create charming and cheeky characters. Originally from Congleton in Cheshire, he is now based in Bath where he works with his little deaf Jack Russell, Holly, on his lap.

For special offers,
chapter samplers,
competitions
and more,
visit . . .

www.quercusbooks.co.uk
@quercuskids